For Susan

MARCUS SEDGWICK

OXFORD
UNIVERSITY PRESS

Great Clarendon Street, Oxford, OX2 6DP, United Kingdom

Oxford University Press is a department of the University of Oxford.

It furthers the University's objective of excellence in research, scholarship, and education by publishing worldwide. Oxford is a registered trade mark of Oxford University Press in the UK and in certain other countries

British Library Cataloguing in Publication Data

Data available

ISBN 978-0-19-8494973

1 3 5 7 9 10 8 6 4 2

Paper used in the production of this book is a natural, recyclable product made from wood grown in sustainable forests.

The manufacturing process conforms to the environmental regulations of the country of origin.

Printed in China by Golden Cup

Acknowledgements

Cover illustration by Carolina Rodriguez Fuenmayor

The publisher would like to thank Liz Miles for writing the additional resources.

Sometimes I see people staring at the scar on the side of my head. I know what they're thinking. They want to ask how I got it. But they don't – they just stare. I try to keep the scar hidden by having my hair long. But there's no hiding the white line that comes over my left ear and down to my cheekbone. And people look but they don't ask.

Other times, they might remember something – if they hear my name, and if they're the right age. My name is ... unusual, after all, and hearing it will start them remembering.

"Porter Fox?" they say. "*The* Porter Fox?"

And I try to smile and say, "No", but I can see they don't believe me. I can see that they are trying to remember the details and so I leave them to whisper behind my back. For I was famous once, for five minutes, at the end of a certain summer.

Over the years I have heard all sorts of versions of what happened. None of them are right, so now I'm going to set it all down. But before you read it, remember this: I only ever tell one lie, and this isn't it. Everything I am about to tell you is exactly what happened. It is the truth.

1

Seven times we looked for them. That first day, the Saturday. We searched that dark place, up and down, back and forth, seven times.

The first time, it seemed like a game. Hunting for them. Like hide and seek. None of us were really taking it seriously – none of us kids, I mean. But a strange look had appeared on the faces of Mr Lindsay and Miss Weston, and it was the same look they both had.

It wasn't the normal way your teacher looks cross, to get you to do something. It was something else. Maybe a lot of things: things like worry, and fear, and confusion.

I think, to start with, confusion was the main thing. There was a question in their minds: how do thirty-four people walk into one end of a tunnel but only thirty-two walk out of the other end?

Because that is what happened.

And if lots of us weren't taking it seriously, our teachers were.

I suppose we thought that the missing two kids were just mucking about: hiding on purpose or up to something. Except, that didn't make sense. Not with the two who were missing. Stephanie. And Stephen. If it had been a couple of the proper "lads" in the class, maybe, but not those two. And the more we searched, the more it became clear to everyone that there wasn't really anywhere to hide in that place.

Lud's Church.

I didn't like it, right from the start. Something about the place made me feel uneasy, but I can't tell you why. I didn't even notice it to start with – I was too busy just being there and trying to avoid Adam Caxton and his mates. And putting up with my friend Sam's endless attempts to be funny. And wondering why Miss Weston from the English department had brought her eight-year-old daughter along with her on our Geography field trip.

But if I had stopped to think for even one second, I would have noticed that the place was unsettling. It was as if there was a low humming sound, the sort of sound that's so low you can't even be sure you're really hearing it, or just feeling it beating at your body. A sound gnawing away at you, one you only notice when it stops. This place was like that.

When we got there, we didn't even know we had. Not at first. It was all so confusing. For one thing, you have to remember how hot it was. That summer, that famous summer. So hot. No rain all year, almost none the previous year.

The sun beat down, day after day. Even before the holidays began, it was super-hot. Now we were back at school, the summer was nearly over, and still it didn't rain. The temperature was in the high twenties every day, then into the low thirties. Rivers dried up and they put in a hosepipe ban, and then they even had to put these little water trucks out in some places. There was one at the end of our street, and me and my little sister would take it in turns to go and line up for drinking water.

By the end of that summer, the ground looked crazy. I'd seen pictures on the TV once of the droughts in Africa, and now our parks and fields looked like that – the grass all dead and the mud dried out and cracked. Cracked in wild patterns.

And there we were, thirty-four of us packed into a bus on a stinking hot day for our Geography trip, and on a Saturday too. I can't remember why it had to be a Saturday but somehow it did. We were only a week or so back into term and we had to give up half our weekend. That was another thing that no one liked.

Across the moors went the bus, and you know there was no such thing as aircon back then. The bus was ancient, and it just had these tiny slits for windows. Half of them wouldn't open at all, so by the time we even arrived at the car park, everyone was in a mean mood.

We crawled off the bus, just hanging out. Then I saw Adam Caxton making faces at me, mouthing things, like how he was going to hurt me next, and I tried to pretend I hadn't seen. But we both knew I had, and there was no avoiding his presence, his bulky strength.

I turned away and heard Mr Lindsay making some arrangements with the bus driver, an old man called Ted who always did stuff for the school. He was ancient too, like his bus. I mean, I suppose he seemed that way to me then, but I liked him. Ted was OK.

"OK, Jim, see you at five," Ted said to Mr Lindsay, and drove off. We were left standing by the ruins of some old mill by the river, while Adam sniggered with his friends because they'd just found out Mr Lindsay was called Jim. What was he supposed to be called? *Idiots*, I remember thinking.

From there, it wasn't really that far to the forest. We just made a meal of it. Dragging along. Thirty-one hot and stupid teenagers. Miss Weston and her daughter were up front. Mr Lindsay came along behind, telling us things about the rocks and the river and the Dark Peak itself.

We walked alongside the River Dane, but there was almost no water in it. With the drought it was no more than a brown trickle between the stones.

Sam and I were near the front, to get away from certain people. We were still near the front when we walked up out of the small valley and into the sloping forest that covered the hillside to our left.

A few minutes later and we were deep into the trees. And then there we were, at the bottom end of Lud's Church. Even then you couldn't see it. Mr Lindsay had to call ahead to Miss Weston because she'd just walked right past it. You could be right at its mouth – the entrance to this place, I mean – but you couldn't see it, not until you took a few more steps and then you were inside.

Mr Lindsay, who must have been there before, made us stand around him in a circle while he gave us a lecture. He told us how it was formed, from the land slipping, from the whole hillside slipping a tiny bit, and opening this crack in the land.

And Mr Lindsay told us when it had happened. It was long ago, but not as long ago as I'd been expecting him to say, though I don't know why I thought that. And then Miss Weston told us one of the stories about the place, which was why she'd come, I guess. She said there was this really old poem, written in English so old you would barely know it was English, and it was about one of King Arthur's knights. She told us that it happened here.

"For real, Miss? King Arthur?" Sam said, and people rolled their eyes. Meanwhile Miss Weston explained that the end of the story was set there. And she made Sam feel better by glaring at everyone else and explaining that, while no one knew for sure, there was every chance that King Arthur had been a real king of Britain, once upon a time and long ago, when it wasn't even called Britain yet. She called the country by another name: Logres. She told us that Arthur was maybe even what we would think of as Welsh, and she told us that the Welsh for England is *Lloegr*, to make her point.

"So why's it called Lud's Church, Miss?" Sam said.

"No one really knows," she replied. "Some people think it was named after a man who was arrested here for his religious beliefs. Other people say that 'Lud' is an old word for 'back' and the forest you are now standing in is called Back Forest. But no one really knows."

"You have twenty minutes to make your way through," said Mr Lindsay, staring at his watch. "Make some notes of the rock structures. You remember from our lesson that this is a Carboniferous sandstone. Yes? Yes."

No one seemed to remember anything of the sort, but we all clutched pencils and notepads anyway, as if we were detectives ready to record something important. I think it's fair to say we were bored. Most of us. If only we had known what was to come.

Mr Lindsay was still giving us instructions. "We will all meet at the top end of the so-called Church, by the edge of the forest, at half past two. Sharp!"

Mr Lindsay was always tough about people being on time. It was his thing.

So we went in.

It's hard to describe. I remember thinking, as I walked inside, it was like one of those cracks in the sun-dried ground of that summer. Imagine you were an insect crawling into such a crack. Imagine you made it ten thousand times bigger, and placed it sloping up a hillside, and then covered it all with a forest of scrubby trees and ferns. That was how I saw it then.

If I think about it now, I imagine the day that God finished making the Earth. I see Him with a giant knife, having shaped and scraped the ball that is our world. Before moving on to decide whether or not to create evil, God makes one final thoughtless action. He stabs the tip of the knife into the ground, here in the Dark Peak. To Him, the peaty soil covering the ground is no more than a thin film of near-black mud. His cosmic knife jabs into the rock below, and then He pulls the knife out again, opening the stone just a fraction. Leaving behind a deep, dark chasm of a place. A tight ravine, with sheer sides, secret and hidden.

That's Lud's Church.

Within a few steps, the walls rose above us rapidly. I had the sense we were gently climbing up, but the walls climbed faster, and soon they towered above our heads, fifty feet, maybe more. It was hard to tell from inside.

The green forest and blue sky had become a thin blur of colour far above our heads as we walked in cool darkness. And the gap along which we were walking was no more than a few feet wide at most.

It took a turn this way and that, and very soon you only saw a few people at once, though there were more than thirty of us in that gap. It was cold. I mean, *really* cold. The terrible heat of that summer was gone in an instant, as if the sun never reached right into the bottom of this dank hole. And so we made our way along and up, dutifully looking at the old rocks all around us, covered in moss, with ferns hanging in great clumps here and there.

Sam and I were somewhere in the middle of the group. Near the end of the Church, Sam stopped and turned around to wait for me. Then he shouted.

"Do you see that? Look! It's a face!"

I looked, but I didn't see it. Some others stopped around us and for one brief moment, other people actually found Sam interesting as he showed how the edges of the rock wall, to one side, looked like a face in profile. And some of us could see it and others couldn't, but those that could said it was cool, or spooky, or both. Like the face of some giant man, with a square chin and brooding eyes.

Sam and I got to the top at half past two exactly. We scrambled up some stone steps that someone had put there to make it a bit easier to climb the final steep section, and there we were. Out of the Church and standing at the top edge of the forest, just as Mr Lindsay had said. Just as he had told us.

*

Except, it wasn't quite as he told us. Mr Lindsay said we would *all* meet at the top. But we didn't.

One by one, we climbed out. Mr Lindsay came last, and he was late, nearly ten minutes late. He checked his watch, as if surprised by something, and then he shook his head. He smiled at Miss Weston.

"There," he said. "Everyone here?"

I remember exactly that he said it like there was no possible way that Miss Weston would answer with anything other than "Yes. All here."

But she didn't.

"Just a couple more." That's what she said, and even then I saw that strange look creep into Mr Lindsay's eyes.

"No," he said. "That's everyone. It must be."

"Thirty-one here," Miss Weston said. "Including you and me."

"Thirty-*one*?" asked Mr Lindsay.

"Well, thirty-two. With Joan."

Joan was her daughter, the little girl.

Mr Lindsay turned sideways, away from most of us kids, and he lowered his voice as he spoke more urgently to Miss Weston. But I heard what he said.

"Which is it, Jessie? Thirty-one or thirty-two? Or thirty-*four*?"

That was how it began.

Then, for hours, we hunted for the missing two up and down that simple chasm of rock, and I saw that strange look spread from Mr Lindsay's face and start to haunt Miss Weston's face too. And as time went on, and we searched and searched again, others began to notice it.

Soon there was no more laughter, no fooling around. Even Sam went quiet, even Adam Caxton and his idiots. As we went on, again and again, we grew tired and hungry and miserable.

Then someone started snivelling. Mr Lindsay turned and snapped at them, and then everyone was totally silent and trudged on without making a sound.

By this time, we had worked out who was missing. It was Stephanie Best. And Stephen Greene. As I said, it made no sense for these two to be missing. They were not the type who go missing. They were not the type who fool around. They didn't even know each other, not in any real way. From time to time Mr Lindsay or Miss

Weston would call out "Stephanie! Stephanie?", but the sound just bounced around the rocks and was soon swallowed. No reply.

And it was strange, but children go missing. It happens. In fact, things only really became strange when one of them was *found*. That was when things really stopped making sense. When they found Stephanie.

2

There were many strange stories connected to Lud's Church, but I didn't know that then. I found some of them out later, but the story most people know is the story of Sir Gawain. This was the story that Miss Weston had told as we stood at the mouth of the chasm. It goes like this.

King Arthur and his knights are at Camelot, feasting. It's Christmas time, New Year's Day, in fact, and for days they have been eating and drinking and boasting about their exploits. Then the doors fly open and in comes a terrible figure. It's a huge man, riding an equally huge horse. He's massive, like a tree, and this is the weird part: just like a tree he is green, from head to foot. His skin and hair are green, his clothes are green, even his horse is green.

Everyone stops and stares as this terrifying character walks over to the banqueting table. He wears no helmet, and his feet are bare, but his clothes are very fine and richly made, with gold trimmings. In one hand he carries a holly branch and in the other, a colossal axe.

This huge man challenges the knights to what he calls a Christmas game. With a deep and frightening voice, he offers his axe to any knight to take one swing at his head with it, on the condition that he will then be allowed one swing at the knight in return. The room is silent. One swing from any of them and the Green Knight will be dead, but he seems strangely untroubled by this fact.

Now all of King Arthur's brave knights appear to have suddenly become cowards. Arthur himself says he will accept the challenge, but then his nephew Sir Gawain begs to take up the game instead, sensing danger. Gawain comes forward and takes the axe from the Green Knight, who calmly kneels before Gawain, baring his green neck.

Gawain swings and, with a single neat blow, cuts the knight's head clean off. Blood spurts across the hall, but the body of the knight doesn't fall. Everyone watches in horror as the body rises to its feet, walks across the room and collects its head where it has fallen. He holds his head aloft, and the eyes open wide and the dreadful voice comes out, just as before.

The Green Knight says he will give Gawain a year of peace, and then Gawain must ride and find him in the place where he lives. There they will complete the game, with one swing of his axe on Gawain's neck.

He leaves, and everyone stares open-mouthed in horror at Gawain. To keep his honour as a knight, in a year's time he must ride and confront his certain death at the place the Green Knight has spoken of. The Green Chapel. Which was, according to the books Miss Weston had read, Lud's Church.

I hadn't paid much attention to the story as she told it to us, but as we went up and down the deep chasm, looking for Stephanie and for Stephen, it began to run around my head again.

The place *was* like a church in some way – like some vast cathedral of stone. A natural cathedral, not one made by human beings. It was silent, like a cathedral, and cold, and had that smell of damp that churches always have.

Churches make you feel powerless, like you are nothing, like you are not important, and cathedrals make you feel that even more. This place was like that too. We were just ants, crawling around, looking for two other ants who had gone missing. The rocks did not care.

The afternoon was wearing on, and people started to talk again. No one was really looking now, not properly – they just sat about and from time to time someone said something stupid. Sam said, "Maybe they climbed out? Up? Out of the sides?" and everyone just stared at him for even thinking it. You could see it was impossible to have done that – even a rock climber with all their gear would have had a hard time of it. Two teenagers in trainers had no chance. But at least Sam was still trying. In one or two places along the chasm there were crevices in the rock, or small recesses, but there was nowhere anyone could hide or go missing – not if you wanted to find them.

Mr Lindsay and Miss Weston kept huddling together and whispering at each other fiercely. Joan, Miss Weston's daughter, hung around. Miss Weston kept trying to get her to go and sit down somewhere, but she wouldn't. She was clinging to her mum, literally holding on to her skirts, like she was a toddler, not an eight-year-old. There was something about that girl, and people called her nasty names. If it was today, they might have known better. And Joan would have had someone sit next to her in class, to help her, because while her mother was a bright woman, that had not passed into Joan. It was like she hadn't grown up beyond a very young age. And God alone knew why Miss Weston had brought her along on this field trip.

Mr Lindsay and Miss Weston seemed to be discussing something. I had the very real sense that they didn't know what to do. They had lost two children, but they still had twenty-nine other children to look after, and Joan. Hours had passed. And we had only searched in the chasm itself, not in the forest around, but then, there was no way Stephanie and Stephen could have got out without anyone seeing.

Then Miss Weston came over to me and Sam.

"Porter, Sam, you are to go to the place where Ted dropped us."

"Who, us, Miss?" asked Sam, who always had the habit of stating the obvious.

"Stop talking and listen, Sam," Miss Weston said. "You two are to go. There was a cottage there – knock at the door and ask to make a phone call. This is the headmaster's home phone number. You are to explain to him what has happened and to ask for his instruction."

Miss Weston handed me a slip of paper with Mr Lammer's phone number. I had never even spoken to our headmaster before, and now I had to phone him. And everyone was terrified of Mr Lammer, even the Adam Caxtons of this world.

As she handed the number to me, I had the weirdest feeling that in that moment something important was happening. That things were changing. I had no idea what.

Miss Weston hadn't finished. And still Joan was clinging to her. And everyone else was watching the whole scene. I felt all their eyes on us.

"Jim ..." Miss Weston continued, "I mean, *Mr Lindsay* and I are going to stay here and talk to everyone and find out who saw Stephanie last. And Stephen, of course."

"Mum!" said Joan suddenly. "I saw them last!"

"Joan, be quiet, will you? Please?"

"But I saw them!" Joan insisted.

"Joan, you were with me," Miss Weston said. "You did not see—"

"Mum, I did," said Joan. She tugged at her mum's hand and pointed back down into the chasm. "I saw them. I did. The little girl was taking them away."

Miss Weston was on the verge of losing her temper with her daughter.

"Joan, we don't have time for this," she told her. "This is serious. People are missing."

There, someone had said the word finally. Missing.

"But, Mum," Joan went on. "I saw them with the little girl, the little white girl."

Everyone stared and then some started sniggering. Miss Weston shouted at her daughter and then she shouted at Sam and me, and we had never seen her shout before. Ever.

So Sam and I set off for the cottage, jogging. Behind us we heard the voice of Mr Lindsay tearing everyone into little pieces and the sound of Joan Weston crying.

"Why us?" said Sam.

We were running along a forest track that wound around the side of the chasm and back down to the valley floor.

"Why me?" said Sam.

"Shut up, Sam," I said. It was still unbearably hot, too hot to run, and Sam kept stopping. At first I stopped when he did.

"We should be calling the police," he said. "Not Lammer the Hammer."

"Sam, shut up and run," I said.

"They don't want to make a scene, that's why," Sam said. "They don't want to be the teachers who called the police on a Geography trip."

"I'm running. It's up to you if you want to keep up," I said, and I set off again, not sure I even knew where this cottage was.

By the time we got to the place where Ted had dropped us, I was a mess, covered in sweat, so much it was stinging my eyes. I had clutched the phone number in my hand the whole way, afraid of dropping it. It was written in biro, but it had started to smudge, and I wasn't sure of one of the numbers. I thought it had been a five, but now it looked like it might have been a nine. I felt sick as I looked around the car park and there was nothing I could see at first but the huge old ruin of the mill by the river. Then, just behind it, I saw a gate and a path, and there was the cottage.

I stumbled up to the door and knocked hard, three times, four.

Nothing. I tried again, still nothing, and then, just as Sam caught up with me, the door opened. There was this old guy standing there, and for a moment we forgot why we had come. He was old, tall and thin, like he was ill or something. Really pale, and his eyes … His eyes felt like knives pointed at you.

I had to force myself to speak, and I found I could only do that by not looking at him. His eyes. Then, once I started, I garbled it all out: how there had been an accident. No, not an accident, but that two kids had gone missing and we had looked for them but now our teachers had told us to come and ask to make a phone call. On and on I went until I stopped and then the man spoke.

"Don't have a telephone," he said. I thought he was winding us up or being mean or something, but Sam tugged my sleeve and looked up at me like I was an idiot.

He spelled it out for me. "Porter, he *does not have* a phone. We need to try somewhere else."

And I was just asking the man where the nearest house with a phone was when we heard a vehicle arriving. It was Ted, already coming back in the bus. He was at least an hour early, and he looked surprised to see only Sam and me, like he was expecting everyone to be back. Ted stared at his watch for a bit, frowning while we tried to explain to him what had happened. When he finally started listening, he was great.

"Don't worry, lads," Ted said. "I'll phone Mr Lammer. There's a pub back on the main road. I'll be five minutes. You two go straight back and tell Mr Lindsay and Miss Weston I'm taking care of it."

I gave Ted the slip of paper, and then he climbed back into the driver's seat and began making a big turn to get the bus out of the car park. He leaned out of the window and shouted at us, because we were just standing there, frozen. I don't know why. I think we were in some kind of shock, or exhausted, or something. Maybe it was the effect of the terrible heat, but it had become very hard to think. To do.

"Hurry, boys!" Ted shouted. "Get going!"

And it was only when we were halfway back that I realised I hadn't told Ted that I didn't know whether one of those numbers was a five or a nine.

3

The way back took us longer. Sam and me.
We could no longer run. Even if the Devil had
appeared behind us, I couldn't have run any more.
So we trudged back beside the near empty river.
Sam couldn't run either, but he seemed to have
re-found his knack for talking all the time, without
end.

We formed a funny pair of friends, Sam and
me. In truth, I know now why we were friends,
but I didn't at the time. We were friends because
we didn't belong. Everyone else in the year had
some group to belong to. Some gang. The girls, the
boys – everyone had a gang to belong to, and Sam
and I didn't.

The only thing we had in common was that
we didn't belong anywhere else – that and the fact
that we were different. Sam because of the thing
with his parents – that he lived with his aunt now.

Me? Me just because of my name. And because I was from somewhere else. I was an incomer. We – my family, I mean – were different.

So Sam and I stuck to each other because there was no one else to stick to. Except, maybe there had been, but I hadn't seen that yet. Not yet. And as we plodded our way back towards the forest, I only wished Sam would shut up for two minutes, that I could find something to say that might make him think. Keep him silent for a second or two. And then something did it for me.

"You hear that?" Sam said, breaking off mid-sentence.

We stopped. I tilted my head to one side, I remember doing that: the action of listening, like how a dog listens.

"Yes," I said.

Sirens.

By the time we got back to the others, the police were already there. They had come up by another path, over the back from Hanging Stone Farm. As we arrived, there were two policemen talking to Mr Lindsay. Miss Weston was sitting with Joan, a little way off. She looked tired. Miss Weston, I mean. The rest of the kids were sitting in groups of threes and fours, no longer searching.

They were trying to keep to the shade of the trees, because although evening was coming, the sun was still strong.

We were suddenly invisible, Sam and me, it seemed. Having done our job, no one paid us any attention. No one except Adam Caxton, who appeared behind us.

"You've done it now," he said. His eyes were tight and his lips curled in that nasty way of his, daring me to answer back.

I knew it was stupid to reply, that I would pay for it later in some dark corner of the school when I wasn't looking out for him. But I replied.

"What do you mean?"

"You called the police," Adam said. "There'll be trouble now."

"No, I didn't. I gave Ted the—"

I didn't have time to finish, because Mr Lindsay was calling me over to where he was talking to the police. I felt my guts turn. I didn't like police. I never had. I always felt guilty if I even saw a policeman look at me – I felt like a criminal.

"This is the boy?" one of the policemen said. I hated him already. He stared down at me, and all I remember thinking is that he was ugly as sin. But you didn't need to be beautiful to be a policeman – you just had to act important.

"Porter Fox?" he said. When he spoke my name, it was just the way Adam Caxton spoke my name. As if it was so weird. So *unusual*.

I nodded.

"Answer the officer, Porter," said Mr Lindsay, but he said it gently. I glanced at him, and I suddenly realised that he was trying to be kind to me. To protect me, even.

"I'm Porter Fox," I said, sounding stupid.

"You went for help?" the policeman asked.

"With Sam Madder," I said, looking behind me. "Yes."

"You were the one who messed up the phone number?"

"No, I ... I ..." I said, trying to explain, but my tongue stuck in my mouth.

"Just as well you did," said Mr Ugly Policeman. And then he looked at Mr Lindsay meaningfully. "Or your driver might have actually phoned your headmaster and not us."

Mr Lindsay's lips went tight, and he looked at the dying grass beneath his feet.

"So," said the policeman, pointing at me and Sam, "these two weren't here when she was found?"

"Found?" I spat out. "Who's been found?"

"You can go," said the policeman to me, "for now."

"Sir, who's been found?" I said. "Stephanie?"

"Yes, Stephanie."

"But how?"

"Not now, Porter," Mr Lindsay said. "Go and wait for your parents. Everyone's parents have been called."

And this was when everything started to really get weird, like I said, when Stephanie was found.

Stephanie Best. Just like every school has an Adam Caxton, every school has a Stephanie Best. From the very first day she walked into the school, she was everyone's favourite. The teachers loved her. The school loved her. Other kids loved her. She had a special group of friends of course, but not just any girl could get into that group – there were a chosen few.

The school said she would be Head Girl when her time came, maybe even in the Lower Sixth, so she could be Head Girl for two years, not just one. That they would change the rules to make that happen. That was how everyone felt about

Stephanie Best, but me? I didn't get it. I mean, she was pretty. She had these long blonde curls that were the first thing you saw about her, and she *was* really pretty. She was tall and thin, but she wasn't excellent at sport, she was just OK, and she wasn't the top of the class, not in any subject. She was just OK in lessons. Yet for some reason, everyone adored her. She was like a queen – like the prize jewel of the school. I never did know why.

And now, "thank God!", she had been found.

Sam and I were mystified. We'd gone for help, after all, but when we got back, no one even thought to tell us that she had been found. Another police car had already driven her away to have her checked over in the hospital in Buxton.

And no one would tell us what had happened, nor how she had been found.

We pestered people, trying to get someone to explain it, but Miss Weston told us to stop bothering everyone. All we could make out was that Stephanie had suddenly reappeared at the top of the Church. No one saw her arrive. One second she wasn't there and the next she was, at the top of the steps that lead up out of the chasm.

"How was she?" I asked. "Where did she go? What happened?"

Sam and I tried to whisper to people, but Miss Weston saw us again and snapped and we backed off. And the only other thing we could find out before my parents arrived to take me home was that Stephanie hadn't yet spoken. Not a single word.

Back at the car park, people were being collected. People's parents arrived and the tiny lane was full of cars getting stuck, people getting angry – with the heat, with the worry. Hot tempers.

Sam's aunt came and he left. He didn't switch talking from me to his aunt – he just kept up the same flow as he got in her car and they went.

Then my parents were there, and just as I was about to go I realised something. The car park was full of kids and their parents. The policemen who'd spoken to me were there. Mr Lindsay, Miss Weston, Joan. Something was not right.

I went up to Mr Lindsay, who was talking to a group of parents, and I could see he had his hands full. He was talking fast and apologising and trying to be reassuring. He kept saying, "Everything is OK now, everything is OK now."

But it wasn't OK.

"Mr Lindsay," I said, and he ignored me. I tried again and he still ignored me, and then I actually tugged the sleeve of his shirt. I remember how wet it was.

He turned away from the parents and stared at me as if I was a creature from another world.

"But what about Stephen?" I asked.

Still he stared at me.

"Stephen?" Mr Lindsay said.

"Yes, Stephen Greene is still missing. Isn't he?"

"Oh, er, yes," he said, "but the police will go on looking for him."

"But the police are here," I said, and pointed at the two men who'd been up in the forest.

"Yes, but others are coming. Later. Soon. They'll look for Stephen."

I wanted to say more, but I didn't know how. I was just a kid, and Mr Lindsay was my teacher, but I knew something was wrong. I felt like I'd had to shake myself awake just to think of Stephen. Like when you get up in the morning and you're still half asleep and you're forgetting a dream you had. You have to force yourself to remember it. It was like that. As if we were forgetting that Stephen was still missing.

"Your parents are waiting, Porter," Mr Lindsay said. "I suggest you go home."

"But we ought to go on looking," I said. "We ought to help too, we ought to go on looking."

"Porter, go home," said Mr Lindsay.

"They've found Stephanie," one of the parents said to me, slowly, as if I was simple. As if that explained everything. As if that were *enough*.

I seemed to be the only one who saw it. Before Stephanie was found, the tension had been unbearable. The worry on Miss Weston's face. The same look and more on Mr Lindsay's. But by the time Sam and I had returned and Stephanie had been found, the mood was different. Not happy, of course, but … easier. People were tired, edgy, but not frantic. They were eager to leave, and everything was OK now because Stephanie had been found.

"Porter," Mr Lindsay said one last time, "the police are going to look for Stephen."

So I left, but I was thinking, yes, but why aren't they looking for him *now*?

*

I turned and saw my mum waving. Dad was having trouble turning the car around and people were getting impatient. Mum wanted me to hurry, I saw – Mum and Dad never liked to be the ones to make trouble or be accused of making trouble. So I left too. I was in the car and winding the window down to get some more air when a face suddenly appeared at the opening.

It was Joan.

"Your name's Porter," she said, grinning at me. Then she said, "It was the white girl."

I could see she had slipped from her mother's grasp for a few seconds. Miss Weston was marching up behind her with a look on her face. I had only seconds.

"What do you mean?" I asked. "What white girl?"

"It was the white girl who took them away," Joan said. "So it must have been the white girl who brought Stephanie back."

"What?" I said.

Joan grinned at me.

"She took them down the other path."

Then Miss Weston was there.

"Mr Fox, Mrs Fox," she said. "Porter. Please pay no attention to my silly daughter."

Miss Weston took Joan by the arm and pulled her gently away, smiling as she did, but it was like no smile I had ever seen before. It was full of other things, things that you don't smile at. It's taken me half a lifetime to begin to work out what that smile meant.

4

Now there was a horrible time – of waiting. When we got home, Mum gave me something to eat and then made me go to my room and rest. It was like lying in an oven. The sun hadn't set – it was still so hot. The room was airless and still, and the house quiet. It was during those long hours, lying on my bed, that I realised there was someone in our year who was even more alone than Sam and me. It was Stephen. I lay there for hours, wondering about him and what it was that made him different.

No one paid Stephen Greene any attention. And if they did, it was only when someone made fun of him or bullied him. The rest of the time he was just this quiet, skinny kid, pale like a ghost. And if a teacher asked him something in class, he would always give the right answer. He was that kid the teacher goes to when they're fed up with waiting for someone else to have a thought in their head. It didn't matter what subject, Stephen would always give the right answer, and sometimes that got him in trouble. People hated it if you were smart in that school. I never understood that, but I understood it was smart to play dumb sometimes. Give a wrong answer on purpose so I wouldn't have to face Adam Caxton in a corridor later with his tongue or his fists.

But Stephen wasn't like that – it was like he didn't understand the rules of the game. And otherwise he just sat in some corner, looking at the teacher when he was told to and doodling on the covers of his exercise books when he wasn't. I can still see the covers now, these fantastic crazy spirals and circles and lines, all in green ink, across all of his exercise books. I remember he always used green ink – it was always all over his hands. And he would stare into space, like most of his mind was somewhere else, and he only needed a part of it to say "1492" to the teacher, or "x=b squared" or whatever it was.

But for all Stephen's oddness, there was no reason not to be looking for him. Mum came up to see me before I went to sleep, and I asked why no one was looking for him. She said they were.

"But not properly," I said. "Not properly."

And she told me to go to sleep and stop worrying about the way some things were in the world. That we had plenty of trouble as it was. That there was nothing I could do to change people.

The following day, Sunday, dragged by. Sam was my only friend, but I had no way of speaking to him. I didn't know his phone number, and we never saw each other out of school. I didn't even know exactly where he lived, but I knew it was miles from me, too far to cycle, even if I'd known where to go. And it was still so very hot.

I kicked a football against the back wall of the house for ten minutes, and then the heat got to me and I spent the rest of the day staring at the TV. I had no idea what was on, until suddenly it went to the local news and there was this reporter standing at the entrance to Lud's Church.

It was like someone punched me in the stomach. I'd been half asleep and then, the moment I saw that place, I was sitting forward, feeling like I wanted to be sick. This smarmy idiot was talking about how Stephanie Best and "a boy" from our school had gone missing, but how, happily, Stephanie had been found. Just before the item finished, he said, "The search continues for the other 'student'," like it was the least important part of the whole story. And then I thought about Stephen alone in that place overnight.

School was weird. Of course, there were no mobile phones back then, no messaging apps. No social media to post things on, nowhere to say "We're all so glad that Stephanie has been found". Nothing like that, to show how great you are, what an amazing human being. But despite that, everyone knew about the trip.

Everyone knew, but no one would speak about it. And I mean, *no one*. It was as if someone had passed a law not to talk about the trip, or Stephanie. Especially not Stephen. I don't know how this happened, if someone organised it. Perhaps Mr Lammer had terrified all the teachers into terrifying the students into silence. However it happened, no one said anything about the trip. It was as if a spell had been cast over the whole school, like in a fairy tale. Everyone went to lessons and answered questions and handed in their homework, but it wasn't normal. Everything was just too quiet, as if everyone was in some kind of trance. Some kind of bad dream.

Stephanie herself had been given a few days off school. I hadn't seen Sam all morning – we were in different lessons. At lunchtime, I headed for the library. I did this a lot anyway – it was a safe place for the simple reason that Adam Caxton would never enter a library unless he was forced to for a lesson. But this time I had a reason to go. I searched though the small boxes of cards trying to find the book I wanted and where it would be kept. But when I went to the shelves it wasn't there.

"You looking for this?"

I turned and there was Sam, down one of the stacks, holding the book I was after.

"Don't bother," Sam said, "you can't read any of it."

He held it out to me, and I looked at the cover. *Sir Gawain and the Green Knight*.

I flicked it open and read a few lines at random:

Loke, Gawan, thou be graythe to go as thou hettez,
And layte as lelly til thou me, lude, fynde.

41

"This is English?" I said to Sam. I read some more:

The knight tok gates straunge,
In mony a bonk unbene,
His cher ful oft con change,
That chapel er he myght sene.

"It says it's called Middle English," Sam said. "It's seven hundred years old. No one knows who wrote it."

I shook my head. It was another moment in the whole tale when I felt time slow down. It seems stupid to say it. I was just looking at some words, old words, but just words. Yet they seemed to have something inside them that was ... I don't know. Powerful. Maybe even magical. I know it sounds stupid.

"I'm going to town," said Sam. "To the public library. I wanted to find a book of local history or something, but they don't have anything here."

"I'm coming too," I said.

Sam and I missed afternoon school, or half of it anyway. We didn't mean to, but we just lost track of time, somehow, in the library in town.

We'd been in there for a while when the woman behind the desk came up to us. She had a hard look on her face. I suppose she thought we were up to something, but then I explained we wanted books that had stories about Lud's Church and she changed completely. She went away and came straight back with a couple of books, then she came back twice more, till we had a stack of things to look at.

The librarian left us to it. I suppose she thought we were doing a project for school, and I guessed she hadn't watched the local TV news on Sunday as I had. Not everyone knew about the trip yet, about Stephen.

When we saw the time, we knew we'd be in trouble. We'd missed most of Mr Lindsay's Geography lesson. But we were halfway through one huge section in a book about Lud's Church, so Sam went to the woman at the desk and paid to have it photocopied. That was expensive, but we knew we had to finish it.

As we walked into class Mr Lindsay said, "Boys, I'm going to have to send you to see the Head", but it was odd. He wasn't really angry. He spoke like he was in a daze. And after the lesson we went to see Lammer, and his secretary showed us in. He told us off, of course, and droned on about "personal responsibility" for a while, and then he sent us away. But we didn't even get a detention. Nothing.

"Did I miss something in there?" said Sam, and I just shook my head, bewildered. And I *was* bewildered by what was happening at school, but I was more bewildered by what we'd read in the library about Lud's Church.

Last period was English, with Miss Weston, as Fate would have it. And she wasn't right, either. She told us we were going to read for the whole lesson, in silence, and that suited me, because it gave me time to think. We took out our copies of *To Kill A Mockingbird*. I thought that was a good book, but I didn't read. I thought about what Sam and I had found in the library.

Most of the books talked about the story of Gawain. But there were other tales from all across history. It seemed that Lud's Church was a magnet for weirdness. There was one story that said the ghosts of World War Two bomber pilots had been seen in the area, just above Back Forest, on the hill. And then there were much older stories, like one about a family of cannibals who lived nearby, who drugged travellers and then put them in pies. And another tale about how a mermaid lived in the River Dane and would drag men to their deaths.

I showed that to Sam and he said, "That's stupid – mermaids live in the sea. Everyone knows that." But I read some more and it turned out that the "mer" bit doesn't mean "sea" like the French word it looks like. "Mer" comes from Old English – it was "mere" and it means a pool of water. And freshwater mermaids are dangerous, the book said.

I was struck by the idea that words contain messages, that they contain history. And that maybe names do too. If only we knew how to read them properly.

Then there was a story from less than a hundred years ago, about the baronet of the nearby manor who once owned all the land around Lud's Church. This book said that there used to be an opening near one end of the chasm into a huge cave – one of the largest cave systems ever found in England. And I started to get excited because I wondered if Stephen had found his way in there. But then the book said that the baronet had had the entrance to the cave blown up with a huge stack of dynamite, sealing it for ever. That seemed weird, but the reason the book said he did it was weirder still. The baronet did it because there was a story that inside the cave system lived "a strange and distinct race of beings". When I read that, I felt the skin along the back of my neck tighten and itch.

I thought about Joan. About what she'd said.

I stared at Miss Weston. Her head was bowed over some books, marking, but her pen didn't move for ages. She would make one little mark, and then just freeze again, for ages. At lunch, Sam had told me that someone had told him that the reason she'd brought Joan along on the trip was because she didn't have a husband. Joan didn't have a father, and Miss Weston's babysitting plans for that Saturday had fallen through, which was why she'd had to bring her daughter along. That was a big deal, back then, Joan not having a father. Something you had to be ashamed of. So Joan was something Miss Weston had to sort of hide from everyone.

But I remembered what Joan had said.

That the "white girl" had taken Stephanie and Stephen away. Down the other path.

But I didn't remember any other path – there was just the single one, right along the whole ravine. So I took a scrap of paper and wrote on it and passed it to Sam, who was next to me.

Was there a second path in the Church?

He scribbled and passed it back.

I didn't see one. But ...

Sam wasn't reading *Mockingbird* either – he had it open, but inside it he was reading the photocopied sheets we'd brought back from the library. He underlined something on one page in pencil and then slid it to me.

I read that at the top end of the Church, the path split into two. And that the opening to the cave system, the one that had been blown up by the baronet, had been at the end of this *second path*.

But that wasn't the bit that really got to me. The bit that really got to me was how, once upon a time, someone had placed the statue of a young woman in a recess in the rock, near one end of the chasm. The locals called her "the white girl".

5

Five days passed, and I kept waiting for news of Stephen. They had to find him. It simply was not possible that he had disappeared. I said so to Sam one day and he agreed.

"Right," he said. "I mean, at least they have to find his body."

I stared at Sam, horrified, and he did this thing with his head that he would do when he knew he was in trouble, like he sort of nodded his head. Only it didn't mean he was agreeing with you, it meant he knew someone was upset with him.

"Porter, it's been five days," Sam said. "Five nights. Think about it."

"OK," I said. "But you can survive without food for much longer than that. Can't you? I think you can. And it's not cold weather. There's water in the river to drink."

Sam rolled his eyes at me.

"If he's drinking water in the river," he said, "then why hasn't he just marched back to the main road for someone to find him, stupid?"

I didn't get angry with Sam for calling me that. I was being stupid, and I knew it. But I didn't understand anything, and the thing I didn't understand the most was why no one was looking for Stephen. I told Sam so.

"But they are looking for him," he said.

"That's what my mum says," I replied.

Sam didn't answer for a moment, and then he said, "You're right, they're not *really* looking for him. My aunt says someone in the shop told her that the police are about to call off the search. It's not right, Porter. It's not *fair*."

We agreed about that. That it wasn't fair, that it was just *wrong*, and I think that was when we got the idea that we had to go back, ourselves. If no one else would, we would.

If that was what started it, it was what happened later that day that fixed it. Sam and I agreed to meet at the library in town again, at lunchtime, to see if there was anything else we'd missed, to photocopy the Ordnance Survey map, and to make a plan. But we never got there.

We were in the High Street when we saw Stephanie going into Lipton's. She still hadn't come back to school. And here she was shopping with a woman who had to be her mother, we guessed. She probably didn't want to leave Stephanie alone at home.

Sam and I followed her inside, and trailed after her and her mother for a while. I don't know what we wanted with Stephanie, but she was the closest link to Stephen. Perhaps she knew something. It seemed unlikely, and yet I knew we had to speak to her. But something told us to be careful, and even talkative Sam sensed it. We were both quiet and trailed around the supermarket, just watching her.

It was hard to believe it was Stephanie Best. She looked the same, sort of, but there was something about her that had changed. It was as if the life had been sucked out of her. As we trailed her, she trailed after her mother, who kept stopping now and again to tell Stephanie to stay next to her, to keep up.

Then, when her mother got in the queue to pay, she got talking to someone and we saw our chance. Stephanie was standing at the end of an aisle, and as we approached I saw her just staring out of the window at the front of the supermarket. It looked like she was seeing something else – not the High Street, but something somewhere else.

"Stephanie?" I said.

She turned to look at me, slowly, as if she was half asleep.

"Stephanie, you know me. Porter?"

She gave a slight nod of her head.

"And Sam," I added.

Sam had never been quieter in his life. I don't suppose he had ever stood so close to someone as beautiful as Stephanie Best, never mind talked to her. Not that he was doing any talking. And she *was* beautiful, somehow more so now than before. Before Stephanie had just been pretty, but now there was something about her eyes that made you feel like your legs were melting. But her ... personality ... who she was ... it had gone. That's all I can say.

"Stephanie?" I said. "What happened? Did you see Stephen?"

She didn't answer. She didn't seem bothered by us asking her questions, but she just stood there, looking at us. Then her mother saw us and stormed over and started tearing us to bits for upsetting her daughter. She went on and on, even though Stephanie was just standing there, not happy, but not unhappy either.

Her mother dragged her away, with dire warnings for us of what she would do if she caught us bothering Stephanie again.

But as she was going, Stephanie suddenly wrenched her hand free of her mother's and ran back to us. She grabbed my hands and started sobbing, and then she spoke.

"You have to get him out of there," she said, as if begging us, pleading with us. "You have to get him out."

Stephanie's eyes were suddenly full of energy again, but desperate, as if her life was in danger then and there. Her mother hurried back and dragged her away again, and I was just left feeling the touch of her hand on my hand. Despite the relentless heat, it had been as cold as ice.

So we agreed. Sam and me. It was too late to start that day, but we made a plan. We had checked the bus timetables, and there weren't so many buses going down that main road. Even from there it would be quite a long walk, and we needed time.

The following day was Friday, and that was perfect, because we had private study for the first two lessons. We went to school for registration, where things were still weird. Still that same strange atmosphere, of everyone thinking about the same thing, but no one talking about it. It seemed that some kind of bug was going around too, because Adam Caxton was off sick, and a few others too. After registration, Sam and I slipped back to our lockers, where we'd both left clothes to change into. Then Sam hit me with it.

"I'm not coming," he said.

I couldn't believe it.

"What?" I said. "What's wrong? We've planned everything."

He was doing the nodding thing with his head.

"I wasn't always this way," Sam said.

"What are you talking about?" I asked. "We've got everything planned – we've got twenty minutes to get to the bus!"

"I know. I'm sorry. I can't do it."

"But, Sam—"

"Porter, shut up," Sam said. "You have nineteen minutes to make the bus. I can't go. I'm sorry. I wasn't always this way, you know."

"Sam, what are you—"

"Didn't you ever ask yourself why I talk so much?"

That silenced me.

"Here," Sam said. "Take this. It was my dad's – I took it from my aunt's bookshelf. She never lets me touch anything of his, but ..."

He handed me the Ordnance Survey map we needed, the one for Dark Peak.

I took the map and looked at my watch and saw there was nothing to do but go alone. So I went, and I got on the bus with seconds to spare, and I sat thinking about what Sam had said.

I wasn't always this way.

Sam didn't mean that he talked too much. He meant *why* he talked too much. Because he was scared, and I guess if any kid ever had the right to be scared, it was Sam. After what had happened to his parents. Their accident.

On that long bus ride, my head was full of gloomy thoughts. I didn't feel mad at Sam for not coming, but I had no idea what I was going to do by myself. And already I had made a mistake. I hadn't checked the weather forecast.

Maybe I was just a stupid kid, but I think no one checked the weather forecast any more, not that summer. You just knew it was going to be hot, day after day – you just knew it was going to be sunny and far too hot. It hadn't rained in so long, not a drop. It hadn't even been grey or cloudy, not for as long as I could remember. But I did remember how hot it had been in Ted's bus the Saturday before, and so that was how I was dressed: for a dry, hot summer day. I had on thin trainers that I wore for running, and jeans and a T-shirt. I had brought a bag with some food and water. The map. A pen and a pad of paper, even though I had no idea what they were supposed to be for. I had my torch, just in case I found my way into secret caves. But I had not brought a waterproof coat. I had not brought warm clothes, not even a jumper. I think, by that point in the summer, I had forgotten that jumpers even existed. And so I was certainly not prepared for the storms that were to come, but they were coming.

I got off the bus at the pub on the main road and something in the air had already changed. It took me a moment to work out what it was. The temperature had dropped, maybe ten degrees. The air smelled in a way it hadn't smelled in ages. The whole open moor of Dark Peak lay around me, still baking in sun for the moment, but rain was coming, even I could tell that.

I walked as fast I could, taking the road through the tiny village of Flash – just a handful of stone cottages clinging to the moor. I remembered Mr Lindsay telling us on the bus that Saturday that Flash was the highest village in England. I thought about that and I couldn't believe it was only six days ago. It seemed like a different world now.

For a moment, I wondered what I was doing. Why I was doing it. I certainly didn't feel brave – in fact, if I had let myself think it, I was scared. But I went on anyway.

As I left the village, something smacked me in the forehead, right between my eyes. I thought it was a fly or a bee, but when I put my hand up, I felt a drop of water wetting my fingertips.

I looked up at the sky, and one more single raindrop hit my cheek. Clouds had rolled over the hill behind the village, but these two raindrops seemed to have fallen from the clear blue sky. So I hurried on, but it was another half an hour before I reached the car park by the ruined mill.

The sky was dark now. It could barely have been midday, but it had grown really dark, really dark. In the distance I heard the first low rumbles of thunder. But there was nothing I could do but hurry on again, alongside the river, still an empty brown trickle, though not for much longer.

Then I came up into the forest, by the path we had used before, and ran along towards the entrance to the Church. Something stopped me. I don't know if it was the smell, or if I had seen it out of the corner of my eye, but I stopped.

There was a single oak tree at the mouth of the chasm, small but old. A dead fox was hanging from it. At first I thought it was stuck there, somehow, or sleeping, but then I saw that it was dead, hanging from the lowest branch of the tree. Its belly was towards me, open and bloody and sticky, and covered in flies.

I stared, horrified, not just because it was so nasty. It was weird. The dead fox had to have been placed there, even if it had died naturally, and something told me it hadn't. It seemed like a warning – a warning to me, personally. This dead creature. This *fox*.

And then it started to rain.

6

Something told me I was making mistake after mistake, but I didn't stop, didn't go back. It seemed to me that I had to go on now, go forwards, no matter what happened, because I had come this far. Because Stephen was still out here somewhere. And one look at the rain told me not to go out in the open again. I could see, down past the trees, into the open valley below the forest. I could actually see the wall of rain approaching, towards me, across the valley, coming faster than I could run.

Moments before the rain arrived, a sudden gust of wind hit the trees, and they started to buck and thrash as if they had turned into bizarre animals. They bowed and flailed all around me, but it was only for a few seconds and then the rain hit and I had no time to notice anything else.

You have to remember, it hadn't rained in eighteen months by then. Hardly at all. Literally nothing all that summer. I don't know how weather works, but it was as if all that rain had been stored up, somehow, somewhere, and now it came down as if it were attacking the world. The rain was furious, and without thinking further I headed into the mouth of the Church. At first, it made little difference because this was a church without a roof, but then I went further in and the sides of the ravine rose on either side of me, and I was free of the raindrops that had been stinging my bare skin.

At least for a while. Then the rain started to knife down even into the deepest part of the chasm, and the trees that hung over this vast slit in the ground became saturated, and they started to rain on me too. I moved on, and I found a slight overhang, away from the worst of it, but I was still getting wet. Not just from the rain, but now from the moss into which I was pressing myself. I was suddenly creeped out about pushing myself against the rock so closely, as if I was making contact with something it was better not to make contact with.

And I was cold. Already I was shivering, and for the first time in months the heat had gone. In six months, the only other cold I had felt had been Stephanie's hand, and now this place, this church, *these stones*, were sucking the heat from me. I was hit by the idea that last Saturday it had only begun to sink its icy claws into me, and that now it intended to finish the job.

If the rain and cold were bad, there was also the darkness. As I said, it can't have been more than midday, but I could barely see. I fished in my bag and pulled out my torch, turned it on.

A weak beam filtered out, but all it showed me was raindrops that seemed like long and thick needles of steel piercing the gloom of the chasm. And they shone in the torchlight, and everything else faded further from view.

I tried coming out from my hiding place to make my way even further into the chasm, but it was no use. I clung back into the rock again and shut the torch off, and then the very worst thing of all hit me. The noise.

Sound was already pounding into me: the roar of the rainstorm, pounding the forest, pummelling the Church, ripping at the trees. Now I heard a scream that sounded like some terrible monster and it took me long seconds to work out that it was a scream of wood – a tree had been ripped from the ground somewhere above my head. Then, on top of all of this chaos and destruction, the thunder arrived.

There was a flash of lightning, and even though I was somewhere in the deepest part of this dank pit, the brightness of it blinded me for a moment. The thunderclap came right after the lightning, and I knew it had hit somewhere very close by. I gave thanks at least for being down here and not out on the hillside where the lightning might have found me.

But it came again and again, those lightning strikes, again and again the thunder right on top of them. With each strike the volume of the rainstorm got louder and louder, going up in sudden shifts as if someone were directing an orchestra of destruction, and I was afraid.

Absurdly, I felt like crying out. Like shouting for help, but I knew that no one would have heard me, even if they were standing a few feet away from me. I was alone, and cold, and I started to think I might die.

I don't know how much time passed. I tried looking at my watch, but the little dark grey numbers were invisible. It was supposed to have a small button you pushed to light up the crystals, but that had never worked, so I tried using my torch on it. But the rain was pelting onto the watch face and dripping into my eyes and I gave it up. *It doesn't matter what time it is*, I suddenly thought. *Why do I care? I'll die when I have to. I'll die when I have to.*

It was at that exact moment that I saw something. At first, I thought I was imagining it, but something made me look up at the crack above my head, and I saw something move. Of course, the whole world was shaking to pieces up there, in the forest, but there was something about this movement that was different. The movement wasn't just the random thrashing of branches and leaves. It was slow, deliberate, moving just in one direction. I thought I had imagined it, but as the next flash of lightning came I was looking right at it – a hunched figure moving along the rim of the Church, up in the forest but right at the edge of the drop into the ravine.

There was something else. At first sight, from the lightning flash, I thought I had seen something about the figure that put the fear of God into me. Then the lightning flashed again. The figure had moved along a little way, moving away from me, but I saw I was right: the figure was green all over.

If you asked me now why I didn't run in the other direction, I could not tell you. For some reason, a terrible anger erupted in me. In an instant, I became as angry as the storm itself, angrier even. I wonder if it was the fear in me. Maybe all that fear suddenly got twisted into another emotion – fury – as I saw something to fix my fury on: this green figure.

It was utterly irrational. But everything had already stopped making sense – it had stopped making sense six days before, when two people had inexplicably gone missing, when one of them was found, when no one seemed to care about the other one. As if Stephen was to be forgotten and left to the stones. So I didn't question my anger, and I didn't stop to think as I suddenly began running, as fast as the dark and the wet would allow me, in the same direction as the figure, heading up, towards the top end of Lud's Church.

I was shouting, and I didn't care that no one could have possibly heard me. I *knew* that the green figure would hear me, I knew that the chasm would hear me, so I ran and I shouted as I ran. Then, in my weak torch beam, I came to a place I didn't recognise.

I was near the top, but suddenly there seemed to be two ways ahead of me. I stopped. I had been up and down the rocks six times that last Saturday. Or seven. I thought I knew every step of the way, every fold in the rock, every turn, but here I was, faced with a split in the rock. There was one way to the left and one to the right, with a widening knife blade of stone rising between them. It was simply impossible we had missed it before. All of us, or maybe I should say *almost* all of us.

I hesitated. I turned around and looked back at the way I had come, as if that would help me, but the way was dark and I saw nothing. Until, that is, another blast of lightning struck the forest and did something I would never have thought possible. The tree that the lightning had hit erupted into a fireball, bursting into wild flames of orange and blue. I suppose, thinking about it now, that the tree had only been rained on for a short time, and that the wood in the forest was sun-baked and tinder-dry. The tree burned, fierce flames licking up into the hissing rainstorm, fire and water. Before the rain put the fire out, I had time to see that face in the rock. The one that Sam had seen, and the others, but that I hadn't.

I saw it now, and they were wrong – it wasn't the face of a giant, it was the face of some kind of god, nothing less, with eyeless sockets that stared blindly at the opposite rock face. Some dreadful guardian of the hole. Its face was lit up by lightning fire, and in that flickering light the face seemed to have come alive, the lips moving, the eye ridges widening.

Then I heard a voice, shouting, and turned, and the green figure was right behind me. And I felt my heart thumping in my chest before I realised that supernatural Green Knights don't hold electric torches, and they don't wear anoraks. But this figure had both, and he was waving his arms at me and shouting. Then he pulled the hood back from where it hung over his face and it was Adam Caxton.

"What are you doing here?" he shouted, and I thought that was obvious, but I answered anyway.

"Looking for Stephen," I shouted back, and then Adam shouted something that didn't make sense.

"Me too," he said.

Adam Caxton hated everyone and everything. He was foul to everyone – he made their lives a misery if they crossed his path. And here he was, in the same drenched forest as me, trying to do the same good thing I was.

"Why don't you have a waterproof?" Adam said. "You're not properly dressed."

I saw that he was wearing proper walking boots, and his torch was a real one for camping, not a stupid pathetic toy like mine. He swung a small rucksack off his back and dug out another anorak.

"Here," Adam said, handing it to me. "For God's sake put this on. I brought it for Stephen, for if I found him. The forecast looked bad."

So someone had looked at what the weather might do. I felt like a dumb little kid, while Adam was well prepared and knew what to do.

I pulled the anorak over my head. Yes, I was already wet through to the bone, but it felt good to have some kind of protection from the rain.

"Have you seen anything?" I shouted.

Adam shook his head.

"Here, get under here, can you?" he shouted, and pointed the way with his torch to a section where the wall overhung the floor of the ravine slightly.

We huddled under there, right next to each other, and even in the moment I thought, *Why is it*

that I am not afraid to be right next to Adam now?
My legs touching his legs, our faces bent together.
Why, when I am always afraid if he's even in the
same room as me?

"I've seen nothing," Adam said. "I came up last night after school. I camped by the river when it got dark and started again this morning. I don't understand it."

Neither did I, but there was something else I didn't understand.

"Why are you doing this?" I asked him.

Adam just looked at me. I can still see his face now, uplit by that yellow torch beam, his eyes still.

"Why are you doing it?" he asked.

"Because ... because it's the right thing to do," I said, and he just nodded.

"Aye," he said.

And then Adam's body and face froze. He was looking behind me, and I saw his mouth fall open, slowly, as he steadily lifted his torch beam to shine onto the rock face, up near the split, high, high up.

"Do you see that?" he said, his voice shaking.

I turned, not wanting to turn, but I turned anyway. There, high up on the rock face, was a figure in white. A white-faced girl, wearing a white dress, hovering, floating.

Then Adam swore, and that brought us back to life, and we scrabbled out from the overhang and tried to run. I saw Adam speeding ahead of me, heading back down the natural stairs of the chasm, and then I slipped on the wet rock, and fell.

As I fell, my head tipped back, and I swear to you I saw an axe blade swinging down at my head.

Then there was nothing.

7

Now I have come to the hardest part of the story to tell. It's not hard because there are things I would rather not say. Like I said, right at the start, I intend to set down the truth here. All of it. But that's exactly why this part is hard. Because it is very difficult for me to know what happened in the time I spent alone in the belly of those stones.

At first, I think I was just surprised at finding myself alive. I still had my eyes shut as thoughts returned to my head, and the first thing I heard was the rain. But now it seemed to be coming from far away, and it sounded muffled, as if I was inside somewhere, but I knew I was outside still. There were still the flashes of lightning and the rumbles of thunder as before, except they had grown weaker now, just a little, and were further apart.

I kept my eyes shut. I was afraid to open them in case of what I saw – in case, when I did, I saw nothing. Everything was black aside from when the lightning struck – I could see that even through my closed eyes.

And I kept my eyes shut, but then I started to talk to myself. I told myself I was in shock, or something like that, and that I had to act, and the first thing I had to do was to open my eyes. When I finally did, I found that I was lying somewhere in the heart of the rocks. I had the strangest sensation of being in three places at once. I was lying on the floor of the chasm, where I had fallen, but at the same time I was lying underground, like the fossil of some repulsive ancient insect trapped on its 300-million-year journey from seabed to sunlight. And I also felt I was floating, in a raindrop suspended on its fall to earth, and was looking down at the Church from a little way above.

I stared out, and strained my eyes to see, but my sight was not working in the way it usually does. I know I will struggle now to explain this, but things came and went before me. I saw things, and they didn't make sense. There was no order to anything, but somehow that didn't matter. Normally, you see things unfold across time, as you walk across a room, or as you watch a show on TV, or as you go through your day. Things happen one after another. Now, they didn't.

The only other way I can explain it is like this. Years after all this happened, I had a car accident – when I had learned to drive but was still young. It wasn't serious, I was just a bit shaken up, but in what can have been no more than a second, or two at most, in the time between seeing the other car about to hit mine, and it hitting, I can only say that time wasn't working the same way. It didn't exist any more. I saw a thousand things in that second, and I saw nothing. I thought a million things, and I thought nothing.

I remember thinking about that strange flow of time in the days and weeks after my car accident, and it wasn't even a bad accident. For the first time in years I remembered Sam, my friend Sam Madder, that goofy kid I'd known in school, and I wondered what went through his parents' minds in those final moments. When they had their accident. I wondered if they had noticed that time had stopped existing, just before it actually did for them. And this is the only way I can explain that time I lay in the rocks.

I felt them looking at me. The rocks, I mean. They were considering me. This strange cleft in the surface of the Earth, a fold in the landscape and a fold in time too. How old were these rocks? Three or four hundred million years? *What does it mean?* I thought, as I lay there. *What does three hundred million years mean? I am fifteen*, I thought. *I have had fifteen years of life.*

I felt both small and mighty as I lay amongst these old, old stones. I knew this place was really a church of some kind, a place that pulled people to it, a place that pulled more than people to it – and that it had always done this. That it always would, until time itself is over, and you know they say that time doesn't really exist. It doesn't in Lud's Church, at least.

And I thought about cathedrals, real ones, the ones made by mortals. The ones that were built a thousand years ago, such a stupid little time ago. Ones that took centuries to build. Cathedrals that someone designed, and only four hundred years later did someone else organise the fitting of the final stone at the tip of the spire.

I wondered if they knew what they had in their hands, those workers on the great cathedrals – of England, of Europe, of the world. The stonemasons – they had no idea what they held in their hands. Back then, in the Middle Ages, unnamed poets were writing in a form of English that no longer exists, and people thought the world was just a few thousand years old. That probably seemed like a long time, for what is the life of one person compared to a stone? So they would have had no idea about the unimaginably ancient rocks they cut from the earth and carved into the shapes with which they built their cathedrals. They would have had no idea how the earth was formed, or what magic had made it, what old powers were lying in it – powers that they now brought into their cities and turned into a place of worship. And who knows what they brought with those stones? What was lurking inside the rocks and transported into the cities of mortal folk?

Yet perhaps just one or two of those stonemasons knew the truth. If you have ever been in a cathedral, you might have noticed some strange things there. Amongst all the carvings in stone of Jesus, or the Saints, or the Virgin, you might have spotted stranger things: carvings of beasts, carvings of trees, carvings of flowers. You might even have seen carvings of faces made out of leaves, or faces vomiting tendrils and leaves – tendrils bursting from their mouths, even bursting from their eyes. Green men.

They're not in every church, not in every cathedral. They say that once there were more of them, the green men, but that many were broken and chipped off in later years, when people grew afraid of their unholy presence. But perhaps the masons who carved those strange faces knew something about the true nature of the forest, about the true age of the stones, and what lies inside them both. Perhaps the poet without a name who wrote Gawain's story knew something about old places too.

These were the thoughts that were in my head – these and other thoughts, such as this: I knew something was coming for me. I knew something was coming to claim me, and that the process had already begun, that the stones had already begun to eat into me. I didn't fight it, because there was nothing I could do. I saw the white girl come and go from my sight as if she was hovering around, waiting for the end, and then I think I started to really go unconscious again.

I felt my body shivering, shaking in fact, from the cold, and my eyes closed again, and I saw nothing. But I thought about the burning tree, the one that had been hit by the lightning, and words came into my head. *Brittened and brent.* Those were the words, *brittened and brent*, and I had no idea what they meant, yet I understood them exactly. That was what had happened to the tree: brittened and brent, as if I could understand a language I had never learned to speak.

Then, once more, there was absolutely nothing.

8

"Not yet, he'll live a while," someone said.

There were two voices, close by, and I was also aware that I was inside, properly inside somewhere. I opened my eyes and saw two faces looking down at me.

Adam, and the old man. The old man from the cottage by the mill, the one who didn't have a phone.

I tried to sit up, and my head pounded. I put my hand to above my left ear and felt a pad of cotton there, a rag or something. I pressed and the pain made me feel sick. There was dried blood on my neck.

"You've given yourself a nasty one," the old man said. "Stay still."

I looked around the room, but gently, my head complaining with every move I made. Now, for the first time, I saw a huge grey dog lying by the fireplace. Some kind of wolfhound.

"Where am I? What happened?" I asked.

"Your pal came to find me," the old man explained. "Said he couldn't lift you. We had a devil of a job getting you back, a devil of a job. Wouldn't have made it if you hadn't been able to walk a bit."

"I walked here?" I asked. I had no memory of that.

"Sort of," said Adam.

It seemed I had been half-conscious, in and out of things, and they had helped me stagger back to the old man's house. But I remembered nothing – I don't even remember being found.

"Who are you?" I asked.

"You just call me Thorlac," the old man said. I had no idea if that was his first name or family name. He still looked terrifying to me, but I was in his house and he had dressed my wound, sort of. I knew they shouldn't have moved me, not with a head wound, but, then again, maybe I'd have died up there if they hadn't.

Then I remembered something else, and the urgency of it pushed away the pain. I sat up suddenly. The wolfhound gazed at me from under its grey eyebrows.

"Stephen!" I said. I looked at Adam, at the old man.

"Aye, your pal's talked to me about young Stephen," Thorlac said.

I opened my mouth to tell him Adam wasn't my friend, then I saw Adam's face. I knew he was thinking the same thing, but that it didn't matter. I shut my mouth.

"Truth is, I already knew, didn't I?" Thorlac went on. "I've had the police in here three times this week. I told 'em to stop looking in my house and start looking in the forest. Here, drink this."

He handed me a glass with a thumb's thickness of something brown in it, and I drank it, then started spluttering and coughing.

"You want another one?" Thorlac said, turning to Adam.

"No thanks, mister," Adam said, half-terrified, and he looked at me choking on the brandy. Normally, this would have been a chance to mock me. But things weren't normal.

Thorlac stared at the side of my head.

"Keep that cloth to it," he said to me, and I pressed the bandage to the wound as much as I could bear.

"Wait here," Thorlac said to us, as if we might just run off, and he left the room. He was gone for a while, and we heard banging in what must have been the kitchen. His house was tiny – on the ground floor it seemed just to be the kitchen and the room we were in, which was a sitting room and some kind of study all in one. I was lying on a beaten-up old sofa, and there was the fireplace, and two tables pushed back to back, piled with books and papers in crazy heaps.

"What time is it?" Adam asked, and nodded at my watch.

"It's gone seven," I said.

It was dark in the room. It was dark outside, the rain still hammering down.

Then we sat in silence for a bit.

I didn't know what to say. I had a hard time looking at Adam's face, because I was so scared of it, normally. But things weren't normal. When I did look at it, I had a hard time connecting that face to the boy I knew at school.

I was wondering something. I wanted to ask Adam something. I wanted to say, "Why do you hate me? Why do you make my life so miserable? What did I ever do to you?" But I didn't say any of those things.

So Adam and I sat in silence, both looking round the strange room. It was full of weird objects: maps with lines drawn across them pinned to walls, a skull of some animal on the mantelpiece.

"Crazy, huh?" said Adam, catching my eye, half a smile on his face.

"Yeah," I agreed. "Yeah, crazy."

I think Adam didn't know what to say to me either. Maybe he was thinking, *Why aren't I being mean to this boy? I always am at school. Why is it different here? Why now?*

Maybe he wasn't thinking any of those things, I don't really know. But I do know that my head at least was full of thoughts about why we treat people differently. Why we treat some people well and others badly, and I like to think that Adam's head was full of the same thoughts.

Then Thorlac came back in with two plates, one for each of us with the worst-looking bacon sandwich on it. We didn't care. We ate hungrily. As I finished, I asked Thorlac about Stephen again.

"He's still out there," I said. "We have to do something."

"I know it," Thorlac said. "Nothing much we can do. Not if the chapel has him."

"The chapel?" I asked.

"Aye. The chapel. Lud's Church."

Thorlac nodded to the wall of the cottage as if we could still see that dank green chasm, and in my mind's eye I still could. All of that terrible place. The ferns, the moss. Just the thought of touching the stones made my head swim, and weirder things too – I felt a fizzing inside my ears, a rumble of low instruments playing buzzing clashing sounds. I forced my mind away from it all.

"There's something in there, isn't there?" I said, and it wasn't really a question. I saw Adam staring at me and I didn't care. "Something bad."

"Not bad," Thorlac said. "But aye, there's something there. Something from before good and bad existed. Something much older than those things. You understand?"

We did not.

"What do you mean?" Adam asked. "You said the chapel 'has' him?"

Thorlac shrugged.

"It may be ..." he said, "it may be that we won't know. It may be that the chapel had plans for him – him and the girl. It wouldn't be the first time. When I said that whatever is there is older than good and bad, maybe that's not right. Maybe it's in a different place to those things. You see?"

No, we did not see.

"Things work differently there," Thorlac said. "Didn't you notice? On that day trip of yours? Maybe someone lost track of time? Maybe someone couldn't count properly? Does any of that sound familiar?"

We knew that it did.

"You take four books about the chapel and see if any two of them even give the same measurements for it. Its length. Its depth. Just you try it! It's not that the people are fools. It's the place. Things work differently there, even ... Even people, they work differently there too."

"Mister ... Thorlac," said Adam. "Is that story about the Green Knight ... is it true?"

The old man turned around in the room a few times, like a dog paces before it lies in its bed. It was as if the question had flummoxed him. It seemed a simple question to us, but not to him.

"Well," Thorlac said, eventually, "all stories are true, aren't they?"

No, I thought. *Not if you tell a lie, not if you make something up.* But I could already see that answer would have meant nothing to Thorlac.

"All stories are true," he continued. "I mean, once they're in someone's head, they're as real as anything else, aren't they? And they start in one person's head, don't they? So the minute … the *very minute* someone thinks up a story, it's true. And ask yourself this: where do they dig them up from? Stories? You think they come out of thin air?"

I could tell Adam wanted to say something else, but Thorlac wasn't finished.

"Listen, lads. Tell me this. How does the brain know different? How do our *minds* know the difference between a so-called story and something that you would say *really* happened? How?"

Thorlac shook his head. We didn't speak. It didn't seem like the right moment to say anything.

"It doesn't, I reckon," Thorlac said quietly. And then he sat down, finally, in a chair by the fireplace, staring at it as if flames were there. Then he swung his gaze round at us both again, with those piercing eyes, like the first day I saw him.

"Why do you think it's called Lud's Church?" Thorlac asked suddenly.

"Oh, no one knows," I said, repeating what Miss Weston had told us, "not really."

He wasn't having it.

"*I* know," Thorlac said, and jabbed a long bony thumb into his chest. "*I* know. All those books, all those great thinkers, the ones that have written about the place. All their crazy explanations for the name! 'Lud' means 'loud' because it's loud when you clap your hands in there! No, it isn't! Have you tried it? Sound dies in the Church, lads, sound dies."

"We were told maybe it was named after someone," I said.

"Walter de Lud-Auk, aye," Thorlac said. "Utter rubbish."

"Or that 'lud' means 'back', and this is Back Forest," Adam added, and I stared at him, amazed he had even been listening to Miss Weston that day.

"More rubbish," growled Thorlac. "All those academics and their papers and their books, and not one of them stops to think what 'lud' means in the old language – in Middle English, I mean. When the poem about Gawain was written. A powerful language that was. A mixture, you see. One part Old English, one part French, and a smattering of words from the far North, from Scandinavia. A strange mixture that, and the three languages had not yet had time to rub off on each other. Get melded into one. Each still had its own flavour, you see? And 'lud', that's an old English word."

"So what does it mean?" I asked.

"This word has many spellings, many. Mostly it was spelled 'led', but sometimes it was spelled 'lud'. For example, it was spelled three times that way in the poem. And it has two meanings. Man. Or knight. So this is the Knight's Chapel. Now tell me what's true and what isn't true, lads. Tell me."

We were silent.

"Why does no one know the meanings of words any more?" Thorlac asked, and he wasn't asking us, he was asking the air, the room. He was asking the Dark Peak. "Words tell their own story – you only have to look inside them. You only have to read them. Properly."

"And names too?" I said, and he looked at me sharply.

"Aye, smart boy. Names too. Our fates are in our names, but no one knows that any more. Just me and Brennan here."

Thorlac rubbed his fingers in the fur of his dog, who'd lifted his head at the sound of his name.

"But …" I said. "We have to do something about Stephen. I mean, if Stephanie came back, then Stephen could too."

"I'm sorry," Thorlac said. "I've already told the police. Three times they came and the first they said they were making 'polite enquiries' and by the end I reckon they were accusing me of something. They insisted on searching the place. Said they're not done with me."

I thought about my brief encounter with that policeman and I imagined how rough it would be to have them accuse you of something like that. An old man. A young boy.

"And I told them all I know," Thorlac went on. "I told them. If the chapel has him, I said, nowt we can do about it. They didn't like that answer much, but what could I say but the truth?"

"Do you think there are caves in there? Like they say?" I asked. "Could Stephen be lost in the caves?"

It seemed to me there was a chance of that. He was a skinny kid – he might have found his way into a cave system and got lost, and he could easily still be alive. In my head I suddenly saw him, lost in the dark, for six days, with no idea of where to go, with no light, nothing for his eyes to grasp hold of. It was a terrible idea.

"Yeah," said Adam. "Stephen could be in the caves."

"I think it may not be as simple as that," Thorlac said.

"But what does the chapel want with him?" I asked.

He shrugged.

"It just wanted him, and the girl too, it seems," Thorlac said. "It let her go, but it didn't let him go. I think it only opens up at certain times. When it does, there are signs."

"What signs?" I asked.

"There have been different things," Thorlac said, "over the years. The main one is the white girl."

"But we saw her!" Adam and I shouted as one.

Thorlac froze, staring at us.

"Why in God's name didn't you tell me that?" he said.

"We … We didn't know that—" I started to say.

"I have to be there," Thorlac said, and shot up from his chair, suddenly with the energy of a man half his age. Brennan leapt to his feet, too, and before Adam and I could move, Thorlac left the room. A moment later he returned wearing a huge oilcloth coat and boots, Brennan hugging his heels.

"You two," Thorlac said. "You stay here. Do you hear me? You stay *here*."

And with that, man and dog swept out of the front door in long strides.

Adam and I looked at each other, then he got out of his chair and went to the window. I joined him, and we could see the light from Thorlac's torch swinging as he marched alongside the now raging river, heading back to the woods.

"How does that poem end?" Adam asked me. "What happens to Gawain?"

"I didn't read it," I said quietly. "I couldn't."

"Right," Adam said, and was silent for a moment, staring out into the dark. Then, still without looking at me, he said, "I guess sometimes … sometimes we don't know the end of our stories. We have to make 'em up ourselves."

The light of Thorlac's torch was nearly out of sight.

"We ought to go and phone someone. Our parents," I said. "We ought to go to that pub and do the responsible thing."

Adam looked at me, that half smile on his face again.

"Sod that," he said.

"Right," I said.

And we followed.

9

Those last moments happened so fast – and moments is all they were, compared with rocks that are 300 million years old. Bits of what happened are impressed in my mind for ever – I know I will never be able to forget them, be free of them. Other parts are hazy, indistinct. It's like they are far away, and when I try to bring them closer, they only move further into the distance.

I remember the river. We hurried after Thorlac and his dog, hunting out his wavering torchlight through the rain and the gloom ahead of us, and I was amazed by the change in the river. That brown trickle had turned into a roaring torrent in just a few hours, thunderous and loud as we ran next to it, spilling over its banks onto the path in a couple of places.

We didn't stop. We splashed past, and although Adam had his torch, we stumbled and fell several times, trying to keep up with Thorlac. For an old man, he was moving faster than I thought possible.

"What's he going to do?" I shouted as we turned away from the river and headed up into the forest once more.

"Shut up and run," Adam grunted, and that made me think about Sam. That was just what I had said to him, on this exact spot, exactly six days and one lifetime before.

So we ran, chasing after Thorlac's torch beam like it was a fairy light dancing between the trees. We came along the level path towards the bottom end of the chapel and saw him plunge in without hesitating.

My entire body screamed at me not to go back in there. The wound in my head was singing to me, telling me to stop, and for a moment I slowed down, and Adam did too.

I saw him falter, and I saw him looking at the dead fox, still hanging on the tree. Then I thought about Stephen.

"Come on," I said, and pushed past Adam. My energy made him follow.

Once more, I was in that open cavern, that crack of rock – rocks made so long ago that it was impossible to understand what they were, what

they really were. The sheer walls, so towering
and smooth in places. The blocks of rock looked
as if they might have been made by human hands,
and yet you knew that they weren't. Because that
was what you'd been told, and you believed what
you had been told. The floor, rising in sections
and then with great steps to climb, and all this
in the dark and the rain. Adam slipped once, and
then again. And each time I waited for him to
get up and then we went on, and always the faint
flickering light of Thorlac's torch just around the
next corner.

We were approaching the top end of the
Church now, and both of us slowed again, in fear
of what we might see. I think we had both already
tried to pretend that we hadn't seen the white girl,
but now we were back in the place where it had
happened it was so much harder to pretend.

We turned the corner and knew we were under
the face in the rock, the god face. We hardly dared
to look up, but we did, and there was nothing, no
white girl, but there was the sound of shouting.
And barking. We saw a light through the falling
rain, and heard shouting and barking, and all were
coming from that second path, the one no one had
seen before.

Adam and I had slowed to a walk, and now to a crawl, and we could only move one small step at a time, and each of those took some enormous effort of will to make. One tiny step at a time, Adam just ahead of me, and we started down that second path. It suddenly narrowed for a moment, took a slight turn and then opened up again.

There was Thorlac. Just behind him, crouched on his heels, was Brennan, the wolfhound, barking like mad. Thorlac's arms were raised, and he was shouting. What he shouted, I can't tell you, but I knew he was speaking that older English, the one from seven hundred years before our time, the one that the poem was written in.

It sounded strange to hear someone say the words out loud. It was harsh and hoarse in his throat, yet it was also musical, somehow. The strange sounds bounced out of Thorlac's mouth in a rhythm that somehow seemed familiar to me, even though I understood nothing.

That's not right. I did understand. Without knowing the words, I knew that Thorlac was speaking to the stones, to the rock. He was speaking to the forest. He was asking it, begging it, commanding it, to open up and return the lost boy.

I saw that the light was not coming from Thorlac's torch. Where his torch had gone, I don't know, but the light was coming from a section of the rocks in front of him. Now I start to struggle to explain again, because you know, you have to understand that things work differently in the chapel. They just do. So you have to believe me that that is the best I can do when I say it wasn't as if the rocks were giving out the light, or that the light was shining onto the rocks. There is no other way to explain it, other than to say that the rocks were the light, and that the air was the light, and that Thorlac and Brennan were the light. And then, as Adam and I stepped forward, we were too.

The light was green. Bright green, like when sunlight strikes a deep pool of river water in a mountain forest. Like shining emeralds. We stood in the light. We were it. All of us, as Thorlac kept chanting his ancient words, and I was suddenly filled with an understanding of what is inside every word of our language, be they English, French, Norse: Singing, Chanting, Dreaming. It lasted only a moment, but it was totally beautiful. I felt filled with joy, as if I would laugh with ease for the rest of my life. Then the world seemed to erupt, a volcano of sound opening under our feet, and there was a blast of green energy. In the next moment Thorlac was lying on the rocks next to us, still.

Brennan stopped barking and licked his master's face, but his master didn't move.

In an instant, the sound had stopped. The rain eased to a trickle for the first time since it had begun, and the green light vanished.

Adam ran to Thorlac, crouching down next to him, feeling for a heartbeat, Brennan fussing around. I left them to it. Instead I looked at what had appeared before us: an opening in the rock, just wide enough for me to pass through. Thorlac had opened a strange road, and beyond it I saw a small, skinny figure, standing absolutely still, facing away from me. I knew it was Stephen, and I knew that he needed my help – something was still keeping him there. Stopping Stephen leaving. I stepped towards the slit in the rock, held my breath and stepped through, not knowing if it would close behind me and leave me trapped there too.

The darkness deepened around me. I put my hand on Stephen's arm and spoke.

"Stephen," I whispered, as if I was afraid to be heard by anything other than him, "it's time to go."

He seemed drugged, trapped in a dream-state, and I pulled at him. Stephen began to move then, but still he didn't look at me – his eyes were fixed on a spot ahead of him in the darkness. And I hadn't wanted to look, I knew I shouldn't, but I couldn't stop myself. Despite everything, I made the mistake of looking at what Stephen had been staring at. For all I knew, he had been staring at it for six whole days. The green light. That head. The strange gates. The endless screaming. The faces with tendrils pouring out of the eyeholes. An axe, falling and falling. Abnormal things. Abnormal beings. All of Life.

Then, screaming, I dragged myself back to life, and with one final effort I dragged Stephen backwards, out of the stones, and we collapsed on the rock floor, where I began to cry.

We were still like that when they found the five of us. Adam crouching over Thorlac, Brennan lying at his side, me lying on the rock with Stephen on top of me, my hands frozen to his arms. That was just how they found us.

It was Sam we had to thank, for being found, I mean. After I hadn't come home after school, and when it turned out that Adam hadn't told anyone what he was doing the day before. Lots of people made phone calls, then someone phoned Sam's aunt, and he explained what he and I had planned – what I had gone to do. Then, finally, a full-scale rescue had been put in place.

We rode home in two ambulances, Adam and me and my parents in one, Thorlac and Stephen in another, but even then I wondered who that rescue had been for. Had it finally been for Stephen? Was it for Adam and me? It was certainly not for Thorlac. There were all these people, huddling in the car park by the mill. There were reporters, there were even TV cameras, which was where my five minutes of fame came from.

Who have they come for? I thought. *What do they care about? Who?*

As they were closing the doors on the back of our ambulance, I got a glance of Stephen and Thorlac in theirs. For no more than half a second, I saw one of the things that is imprinted on my mind for ever. Stephen, sitting bolt upright, staring through the air right past Thorlac, who was leaning forward, clutching Stephen's hands in his, clutching them tight, speaking to him urgently. I can't tell you how I know that Thorlac was asking Stephen to tell him what it was like, what it had been like, inside the rock.

Then they shut our doors, and we rumbled back, away from the chapel. My mum asked Adam if anyone had told his parents about where he was, and I could see she was wondering why they weren't there, and he didn't really answer. He just mumbled something, and I knew, I just *knew*, that he didn't have anyone who cared about him. No one.

But no one had died. Two children had gone missing. A girl. And a boy. And one had been quickly found and the other had not, until two kids and an old man wandered out in the thunderstorm that broke the drought and found him. And we were on the news – we were even on the national news, second item after the piece about the end of the drought. But life goes on, and we were soon forgotten about.

*

The rest of that year at school was strange. It's a hazy blur to me now. When it came to sixth form, I decided to go somewhere else, and I wasn't the only one. Sam's aunt took him out of the school a few weeks later, and I never saw him again. I don't really know why. We didn't try to get in touch with each other, and that was that. Mr Lindsay finished the year, and Miss Weston, and they both left, I heard. The story was that they both went to work in a school far away, in the south, and that they were an item. Maybe always had been.

Adam Caxton left school at the end of the year. After that day on the rocks, things had changed. We didn't become friends, but he was no longer awful to me, as before. He kept his distance from everyone, in fact, and stopped hanging out with his old mates.

Adam wasn't the only one who had been changed by that place. Like Stephanie Best. She stayed at the school, but she never made Head Girl. I saw her in town, just once, years later. I barely recognised her – she was pushing a pram, and she seemed happy, but when I tried to speak to her, she didn't say much back. Stephanie didn't seem unhappy in general, or unhappy to see me, but later someone told me that she didn't speak much any more, that she only spoke a word or two at most, ever. But I was glad to have seen her, that she had got married, that she'd become a mother. That was wonderful.

And Stephen? He never spoke again. He had never been talkative, like I said, but he never said another word – he had become totally mute. Like me, he too went off to a different school to do his A Levels, and he passed them all without uttering a word. They had doctors look at him, his parents, and no one could find anything wrong with him. His vocal cords were fine, but they say he never said another word.

Me? What did I do? I don't know what to say, what's important. I lived my life. I grew up, as people do. I worked some. I fell in love, got married. I … I don't know. I want to say something – one small thing, which is this: I lived my life, but I always felt like something was missing. That there was something I didn't know.

Years passed.

One day, as I was walking through Manchester, I was passing the new music venue, the Bridgewater Hall, and I saw a poster for a concert.

I don't know anything about music, but the poster caught my eye because of what it said.

New music. UK premiere of Stephen Greene's acclaimed new opera: "Thorlac".

I went inside and picked up a brochure for the concert, and of course, I saw it was my Stephen Greene. I read the small biography in the programme.

You have to remember that two decades had passed by this time. I knew none of Stephen's history. I read that after school he'd gone to study music. His talent was extraordinary, it seemed, because later he'd moved to New York, where he had rapidly become a celebrated composer. It said he had developed a new style of music, something radical and new.

I bought a ticket on the spot, and I waited for the day to come. I suppose I stupidly thought I'd see Stephen, that he would have come over from New York, but naturally he wasn't there.

Still, I sat in the darkened concert hall, and they were right. His music was like nothing else there had ever been on Earth before. It was strange and uplifting and dark and magical, all at once. It seemed to operate in a different time to normal music, that's all I can say, but I don't know anything about music. And I sat there in the dark, and tears streamed down my face, and I realised in that moment that I hadn't cried that day. I had smashed my head on a rock, leaving me with a scar for life. I had lain semi-conscious in the rain. I had pulled Stephen out of the rocks and set him free. But I didn't cry. And I had grown up, become an adult, and all that time I had never cried. Not once, until the day of the concert.

So why did I cry then?

After all those years, I think something in the music touched me. It reopened old wounds. Some of it was the horror I had seen in that place. Horror that I will not describe, that I cannot describe. Things I had sensed, as much as I had seen. It was all sickening, and yet, there was also a powerful beauty inside the stones – I could see that too, and this was what Stephen had spent six eternal days contemplating. He had spent six days there, where I had spent just a few seconds, and those few seconds have stayed with me my whole life.

That was part of why I cried. And the rest? The rest, I'd cried because I still did not understand why it is that we treat some people well, and others poorly. That was the mystery that had bothered me then and that bothers me still: do we have a choice in how we behave, for better, or worse? Are we controlled by other things, by other people? Even by places?

That is the question I had been asked on the Dark Peak.

And to which, I still have no answer.

out injury
scoe Lane,
the after
were heard
Mr Stones
police were
the source
er time.
ture of this
three men
vening, or
himself
need of a
the matter
ling in the
ger fit for

Local boys are heroes

TWO LOCAL BOYS are being hailed as heroes after finding their friend and classmate who had been lost on the Dark Peak for six days.

Adam Caxton and Porter Fox were helped by a resident of Gradbach, Mr Peter Thorlac, as they hunted in the natural chasm known as Lud's Church during the thunderstorm that brought to an end the record-breaking drought last week.

The missing boy, Stephen Greene, is now recovering in hospital, having been found fully six days after he and another student from the school, Stephanie Best, disappeared during a Geography field trip. Although Stephanie was found later the same day, Stephen remained missing until the heroic exploits of fifteen-year-old Adam and his friend Porter. All the young people are said to be doing well.

The school has been contacted for comment but has not responded at this time to our requests for interview. The reason why Stephen was not found for six days, and his whereabouts in that time, remain a mystery.

Author spotlight

Marcus Sedgwick has written over 40 books for young people and adults. He is the winner of many prizes, most notably the 2014 Michael L. Printz Award, America's most respected prize for writing for teenagers, for his novel *Midwinterblood*. Marcus has also received two further Printz Honors, giving him the most citations to date for the USA's most prestigious prize for writing for young adults. As well as winning the BookTrust Teenage Book Award and the Branford Boase Award in the UK, he has been shortlisted for the Carnegie Medal eight times. He is the UK's nominee for the 2022 Hans Christian Andersen Award.

Marcus was born in a small village in Kent and now lives high on a mountain in the French Alps.

Background to the novel

Summer 1976

The story is set in the summer of 1976. This was the hottest summer in the UK on record, with Mediterranean temperatures of more than 32.2°C (90°F). It was also the driest summer since 1772 with half the usual rainfall. Water stored in lakes and reservoirs soon dried out and the country faced a drought.

There were days when thousands of homes had no tap water and families had to queue to collect water from standpipes or tankers. The government told people to use less water and banned the use of hosepipes. The heat affected farmers' crops, such as potatoes, and some food stocks were low. In the dry heat, dangerous wild fires broke out in forests and moorlands.

The drought finally ended in the last week of August when dramatic thunderstorms brought the first summer rain to many places.

When the main character, Porter Fox, and his class set off to Dark Peak on a bus, it is a "stinking hot day". In parks and fields the grass is "dead and the mud dried out and cracked", and the River Dane has dried to a "brown trickle". At the climax of the story, after eighteen months of no rain, when Porter is deep in a chasm, a storm breaks: "Then the rain started to knife down" and "it … came down as if it were attacking the world".

Lud's Church, Dark Peak

Most of the action in this novel takes place at Lud's Church, which is a real place in a forested hillside in the Peak District National Park, central England. It is an 18-metre-deep chasm, or ravine, in the rock. This area in the Peak District is called the Dark Peak because the high moorland is covered in a thick dark peat, which is a type of soil.

Lud's Church is linked to many magical myths and legends, including the medieval poem "Sir Gawain and the Green Knight", which is a theme throughout the novel. There are different explanations for how Lud's Church got its name, including those suggested by Thorlac (pages 84–5). Another explanation is that it is named after Alice, the granddaughter of a rebel called William de Ludauk, who died during a fight with soldiers. It is said that Alice haunts the chasm as a ghostly white figure.

Sir Gawain and the Green Knight

"Sir Gawain and the Green Knight" is a poem written in the fourteenth century by an unknown author. It is seen as a masterpiece of literature. In the poem, Sir Gawain's bravery, nobility and honesty are tested during his quest to find the Green Chapel and when he meets with the Green Knight.

Miss Weston, one of the teachers, tells the class that Lud's Church is believed to be the "Green Chapel" in the medieval tale of "Sir Gawain and the Green Knight". She tells the first part of the story, in which Sir Gawain takes up the challenge from the Green Knight to swing an axe at his head. The Green Knight survives the blow in spite of being beheaded, and then demands that Gawain agrees to his side of the bargain: to go to the Green Chapel in a year and allow the Green Knight to have one swing at Gawain in return.

Green men

Green men appear in folktales and art around the world. They often symbolise the spirit of nature, rebirth, spring and new growth, and supernatural powers. Green women also exist but are much less common.

In the novel there are references to the Green Knight being green all over. The boy who goes missing is called Stephen Greene and writes with green ink. Porter Fox later describes the "green men" he has seen carved in the stone in churches and cathedrals.

Who's who in this novel

Porter Fox tells the story of what happened in the summer of 1976 when he was fifteen years old. At school, Porter feels different because he is from "somewhere else". He has only one friend and is scared of the school bully, Adam Caxton.

Sam Madder is Porter Fox's only friend and is different, too, because he lives with his aunt after his parents had an accident. He talks all the time and makes endless attempts to be funny.

Adam Caxton is a strong and bulky bully, who uses words and physical violence to hurt Porter. He later proves that he does care for others and reveals that there might be a reason why he behaves the way he does.

Mr Jim Lindsay is the strict Geography teacher who goes on the school trip to Lud's Church. He changes dramatically when things go wrong and he seems to care more about himself than a missing child.

Miss Jessie Weston is from the school's English department and she tells the story of "Sir Gawain and the Green Knight" at Lud's Church. There turns out to be a good reason why she brings her eight-year-old daughter along on the school trip.

Joan Weston is Jessie Weston's eight-year-old daughter but behaves as if she is much younger and gets called "nasty names". At Lud's Church she claims to have seen what happened to the missing children, but her mother won't listen to her.

Stephanie Best is blonde haired, tall and slim, and is everyone's favourite at school. The relief is enormous when Stephanie is found after going missing at Lud's Church, but she isn't the same any more.

Stephen Greene is clever, a loner, and no one really notices him. No one except Porter and Sam seem to care that Stephen is still missing five days after disappearing at Lud's Church.

Mr Lammer is the scary headmaster – also known as Lammer the Hammer.

Thorlac lives in a cottage by the car park in Dark Peak, where Porter and Sam run to phone for help after Stephen and Stephanie go missing. He isn't able to help as he hasn't got a phone, but it turns out that he knows a lot about Lud's Church.

What to read next

Sir Gawain and the Green Knight by Michael Morpurgo

An exciting retelling of the complete fourteenth-century story, from the frightening arrival of the Green Knight to the tests that Sir Gawain goes on to face. The witty and dramatic text captures the magic, monsters, battles and chivalry of the medieval world.

Good Boy by Mal Peet

An unsettling illustrated story in which a monstrous power – in the form of a snarling dog – stalks a girl in her sleep. Her "good boy" pet dog, Rabbie, keeps it away, but when Rabbie is no longer there, Sandie becomes haunted night and day. Written from her point of view as an adult, we discover how fear affects her life.

The Longest Night of Charlie Noon by Christopher Edge

A thought-provoking thriller in which three school friends get lost in a forest and are terrified of the legendary Old Corny, who is said to eat children. Themes include friendship, nature and how echoes of the past can be found in the present.

Revolver by Marcus Sedgwick

A psychological thriller set in the snowy Arctic. In 1910, Sig is left alone with his dead father in the family's cabin while his stepmother and sister go for help. An armed and threatening giant of a man comes to the door, insisting Sig's father has his gold. Held hostage, what will Sig do?

What do you think?

1. At the beginning, Porter says that he will tell us exactly what happened, except that he will tell one lie. What do you think he lied about?

2. Sam is a big talker but says he hasn't always been this way. What do you think changed him?

3. Some people are popular and some people are treated badly in the novel. Who do you think gets the worst treatment?

4. The teachers in this novel behave strangely. Why do you think this is so?

5. By the end of the novel, how does Porter feel about Adam? Have his feelings changed? Why?

Quick quiz

When you have finished reading *Dark Peak*, answer these questions to see how much you can remember about the novel. The answers are on page 123.

1. How many children were on the bus when they set off on the school trip to Dark Peak?

2. Which river did the children walk beside on the way to Lud's Church?

3. Why didn't one of the teachers use a mobile phone to call for help when the children went missing?

4. What type of English was "Sir Gawain and the Green Knight" written in?

5. What was Mr Lindsay always strict about?

6. What is the name of Thorlac's dog?

7. What did Stephen Greene do after he left school?

Word list

baronet: the wife of a baron, landowners who were the lowest rank of noblemen

brooding: showing deep or dark thoughts

cathedral: a main church in a district, headed by a bishop

dire: terrible, urgent

dreadful: causing terror

fate: events that happen outside your control, and had to happen

fossil: the remains or shape of a plant or animal that lived a long time ago

gnawing away: gradually bothering or irritating

honour: respect for others, and an important part of how a medieval knight should behave

irrational: without any reason or sense

knack: special skill or talent

Lipton's: a supermarket chain that changed its name to Presto in the 1980s

made a meal of it: take more time than is necessary

Middle English: a form of English which developed around 1150CE, as the grammar, spelling and pronunciation from Old English changed and took words from Latin and French. Early modern English followed

mystified: confused or puzzled

Ordnance Survey map: a type of detailed map that shows manmade features such as towns and churches, and physical features such as valleys and rivers

pestered: to keep bothering people until they get annoyed

relentless: never stopping or slackening

sandstone: lots of tiny particles on the bed of a river, lake or the sea, which over time cement together

smarmy: being overly nice to people so it seems insincere

snivelling: quietly crying and sniffing

supernatural: linked to forces that are different to natural and explainable forces

Quick quiz answers

1. Thirty-two

2. The River Dane

3. The story is set in 1976 before people had mobile phones

4. Middle English

5. Being on time

6. Brennan

7. He became a composer

Super-Readable
ROLLERCOASTERS

Super-Readable Rollercoasters are an exciting new collection brought to you through a collaboration between Oxford University Press and specialist publisher Barrington Stoke. Written by bestselling and award-winning authors, these titles are intended to engage and enthuse, with themes and issues matched to the readers' age.

The books have been expertly edited to remove any barriers to comprehension and then carefully laid out in Barrington Stoke's dyslexia-friendly font to make them as accessible as possible. Their shorter length allows readers to build confidence and reading stamina while engaging in a gripping, well-told story that will ensure an enjoyable reading experience.

**Other titles available in the
Super-Readable Rollercoasters series:**

Edgar & Adolf by Phil Earle and Michael Wagg
Lightning Strike by Tanya Landman
Rat by Patrice Lawrence
I am the Minotaur by Anthony McGowan
Out of the Rubble by Sally Nicholls

Free online teaching resources accompany all the titles in the Super-Readable Rollercoasters series and are available from:

http://www.oxfordsecondary.com/superreadable